LUKE
ON THE LOOSE

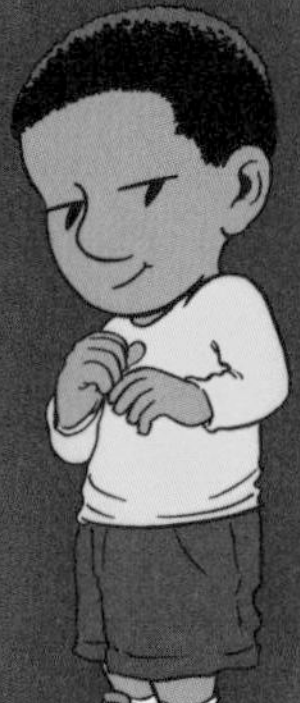

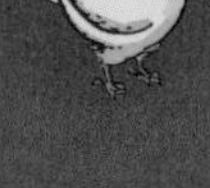

HARRY BLISS

LUKE
ON THE LOOSE

A TOON BOOK BY
HARRY BLISS

TOON BOOKS IS A DIVISION OF RAW JUNIOR, LLC, NEW YORK

For Delia M.

Editorial Director: FRANÇOISE MOULY
Advisor: ART SPIEGELMAN

Book Design: FRANÇOISE MOULY & JONATHAN BENNETT

Colors: FRANÇOISE MOULY & ZEYNEP MEMECAN
Thanks to: LAUREN KAELIN & SASKIA LEGGETT

 Library of Congress Cataloging-in-Publication Data available upon request.

ISBN 13: 978-1-935179-00-9 ISBN 10: 1-935179-00-4

10 9 8 7 6 5 4 3 2 1

www.TOON-BOOKS.com

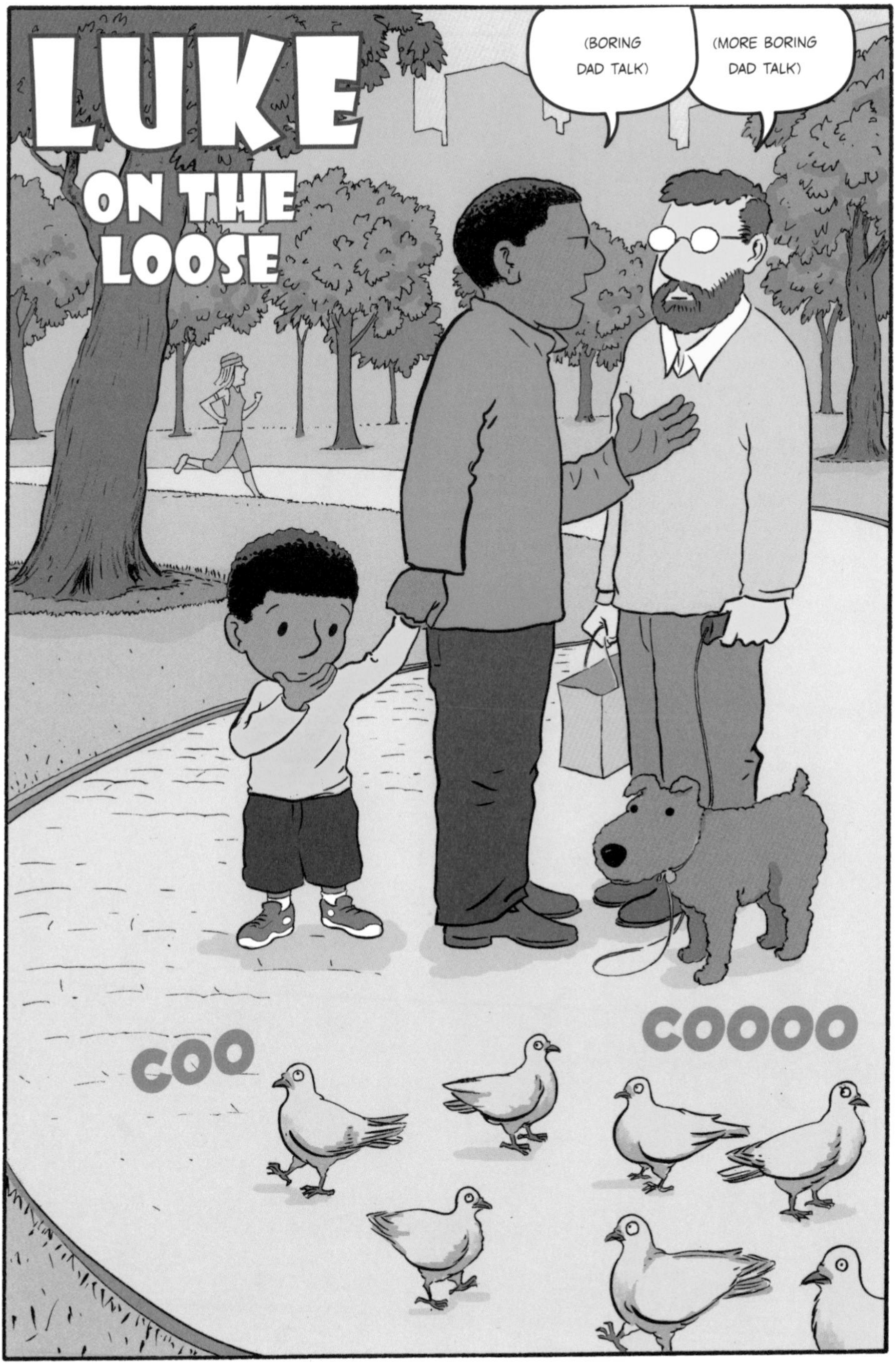
LUKE ON THE LOOSE
(BORING DAD TALK)
(MORE BORING DAD TALK)
COO
COOOO

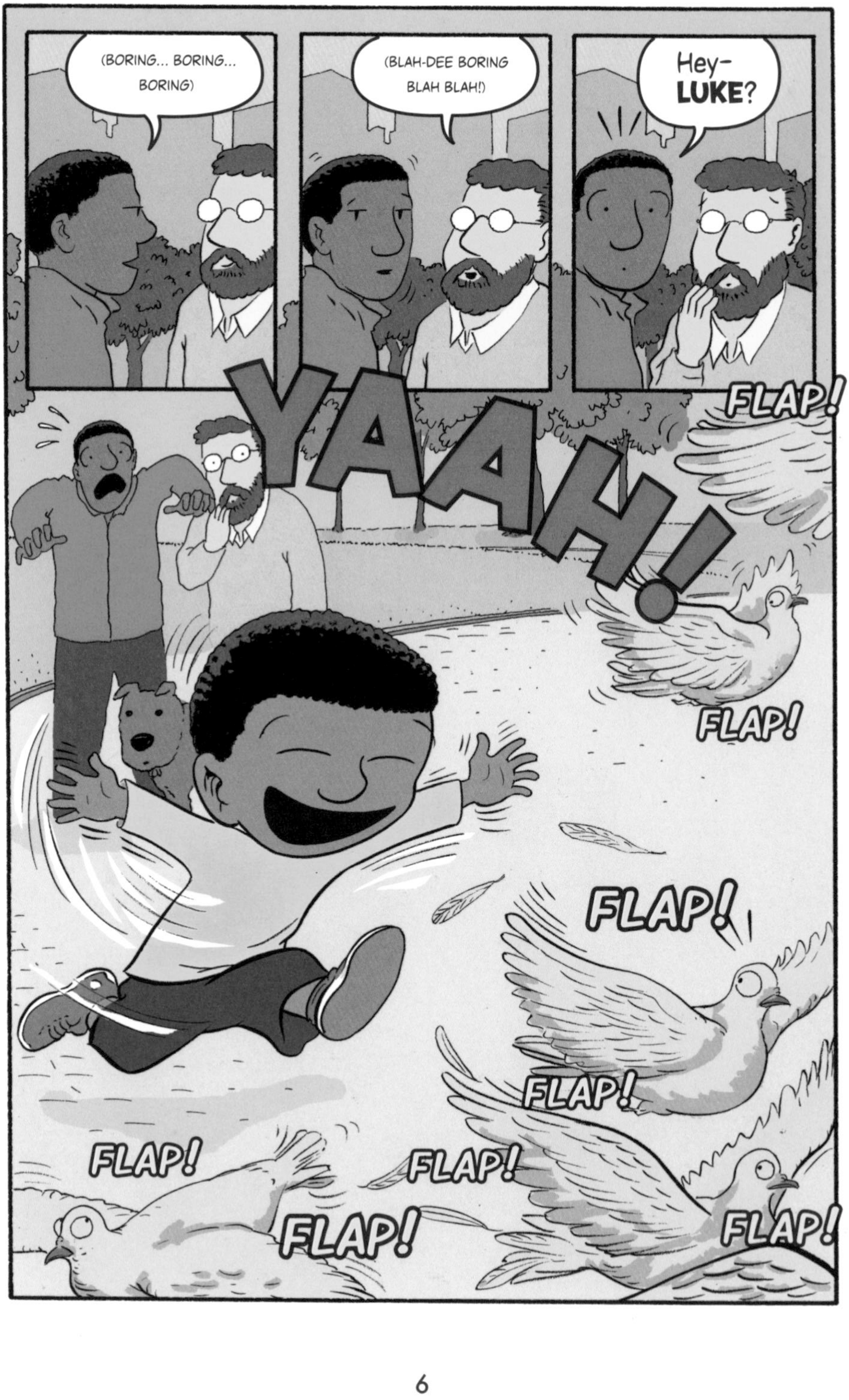
(BORING... BORING... BORING)
(BLAH-DEE BORING BLAH BLAH!)
Hey- LUKE?
YAAAH!
FLAP!
FLAP!
FLAP!
FLAP!
FLAP!
FLAP!
FLAP!
FLAP!

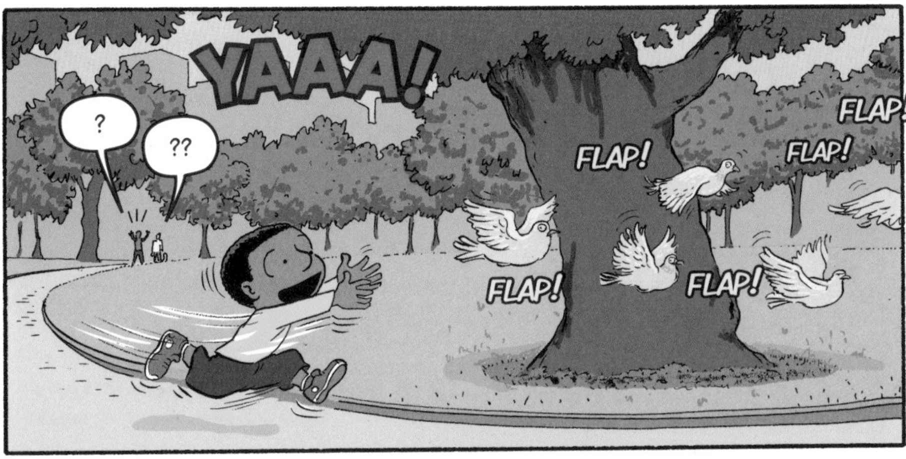
YAAA!
?
??
FLAP!
FLAP!
FLAP!
FLAP!
FLAP!

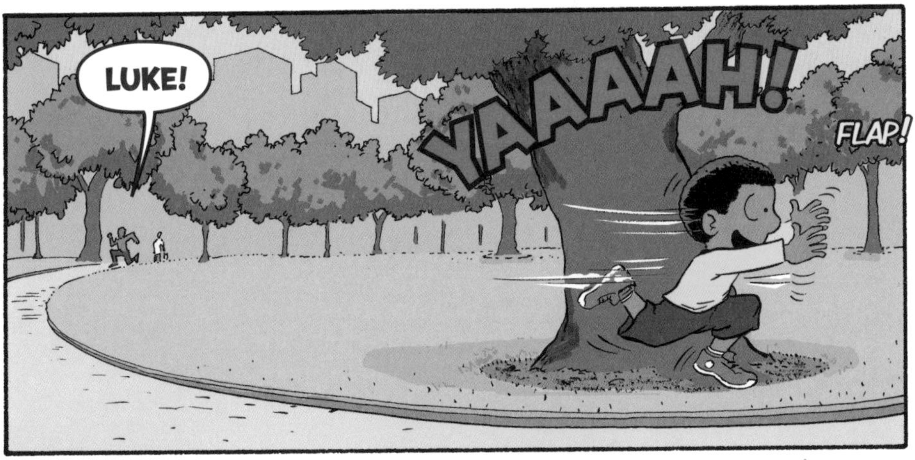
LUKE!
YAAAAAH!
FLAP!

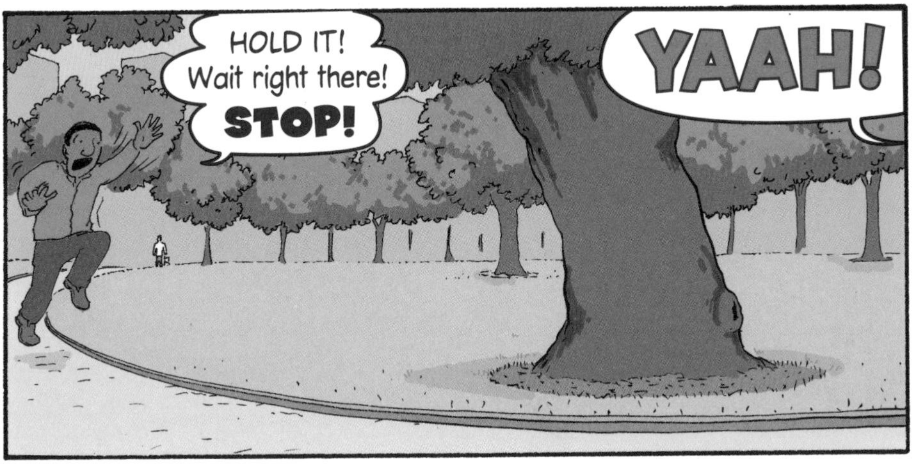
HOLD IT!
Wait right there!
STOP!
YAAH!

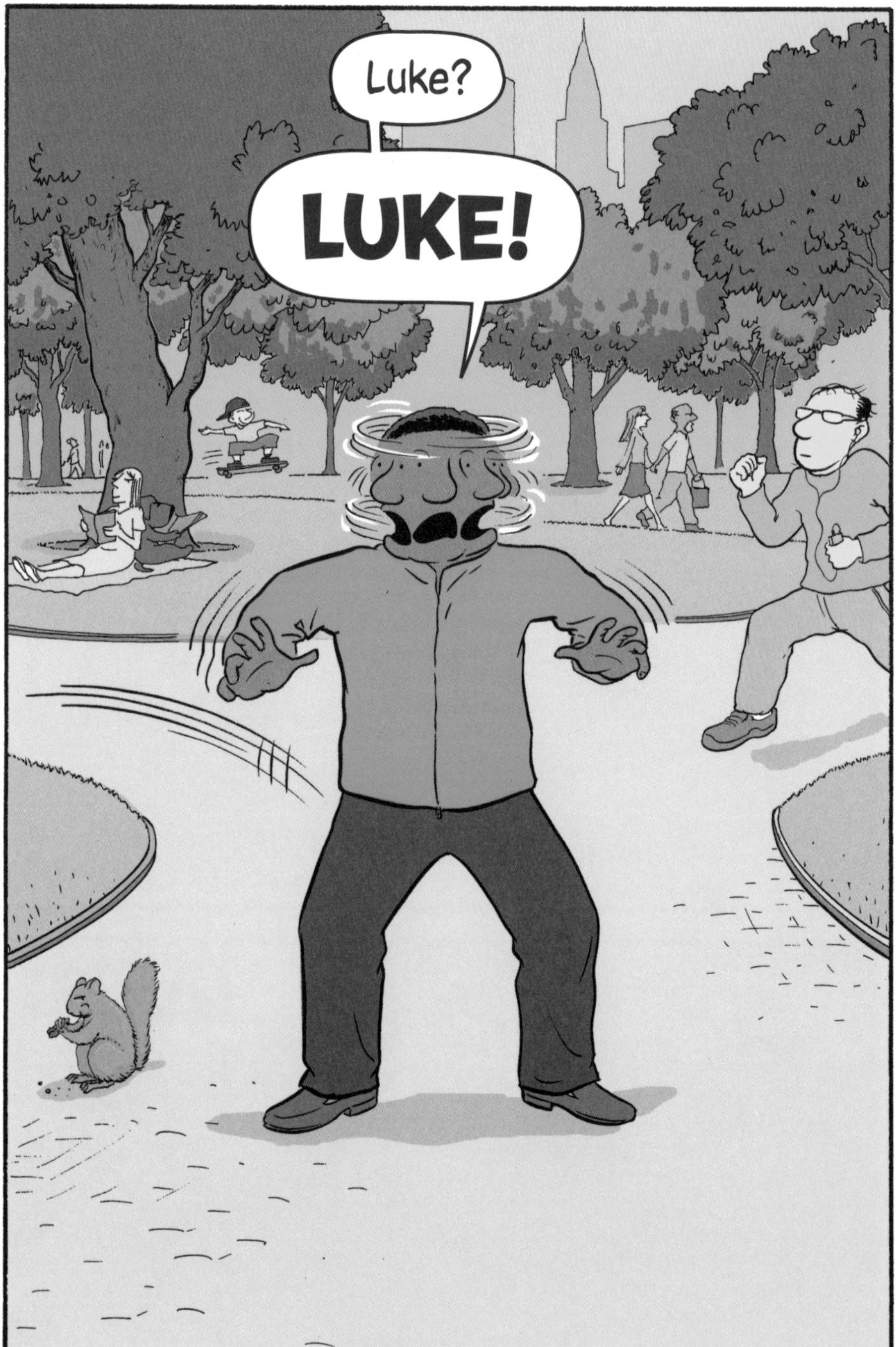
Luke?
LUKE!

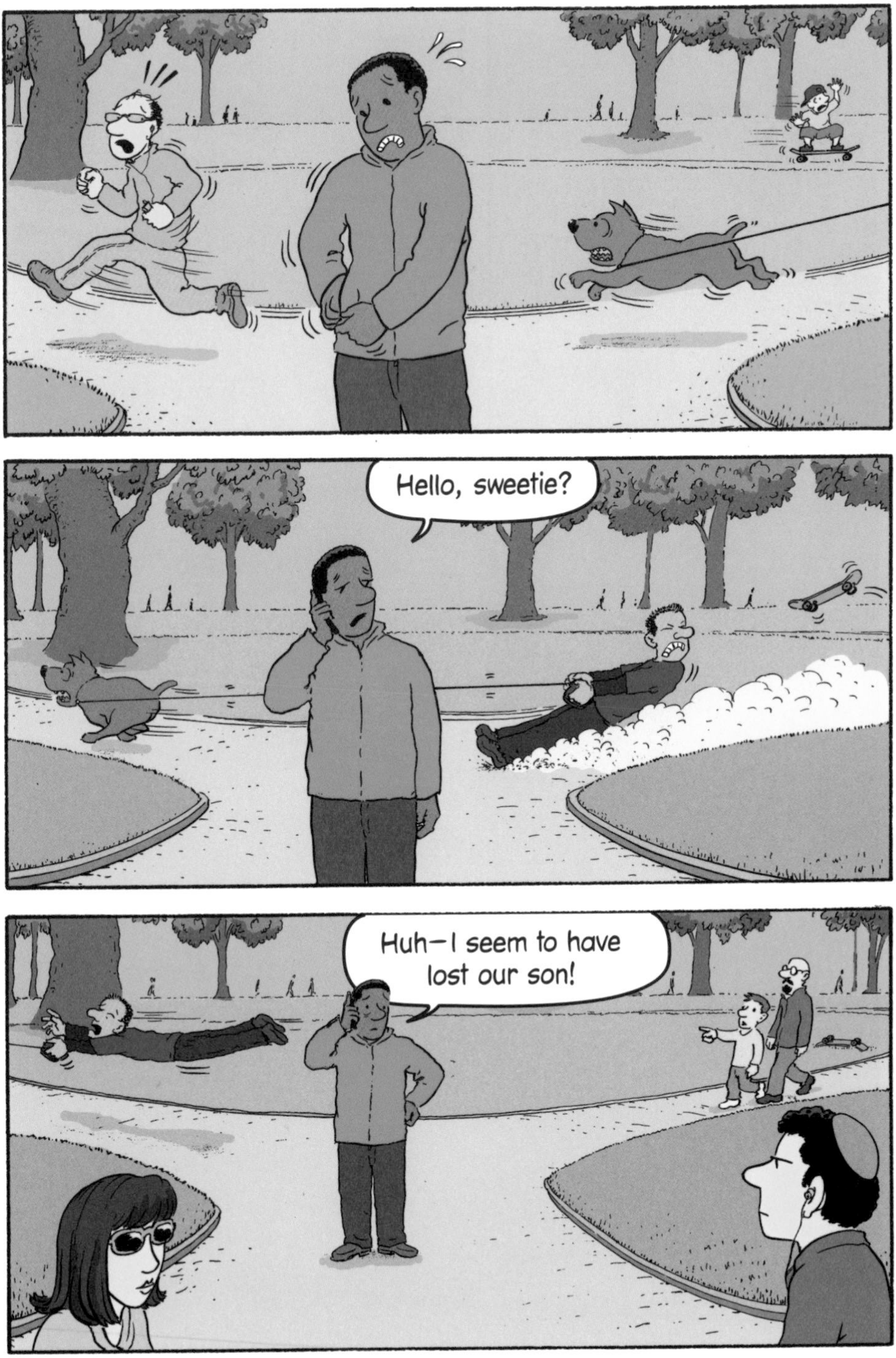
Hello, sweetie?
Huh—I seem to have lost our son!

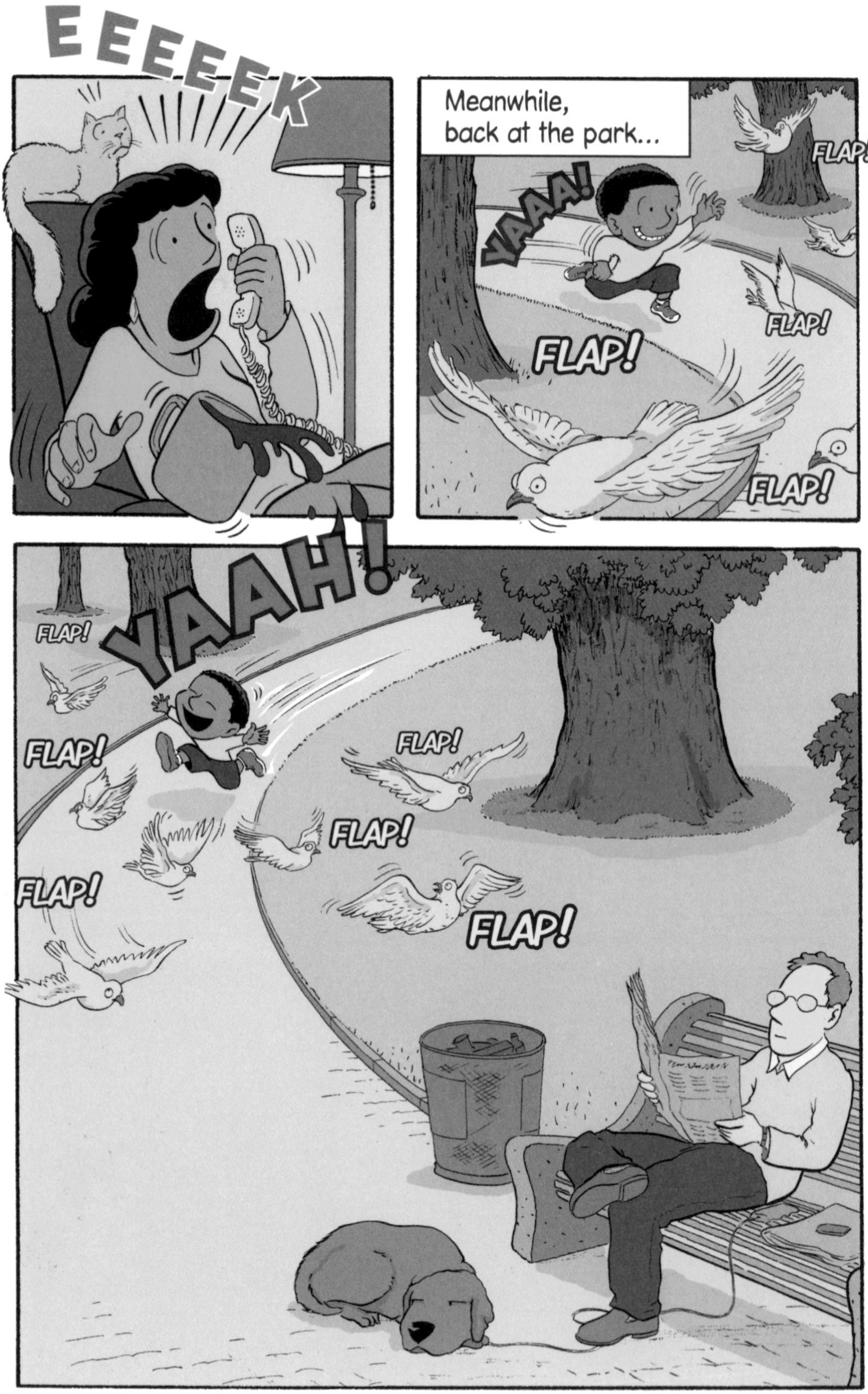
EEEEEK
Meanwhile, back at the park...
YAAAA!
FLAP!
FLAP!
FLAP!
FLAP!
YAAAH!
FLAP!
FLAP!
FLAP!
FLAP!
FLAP!
FLAP!

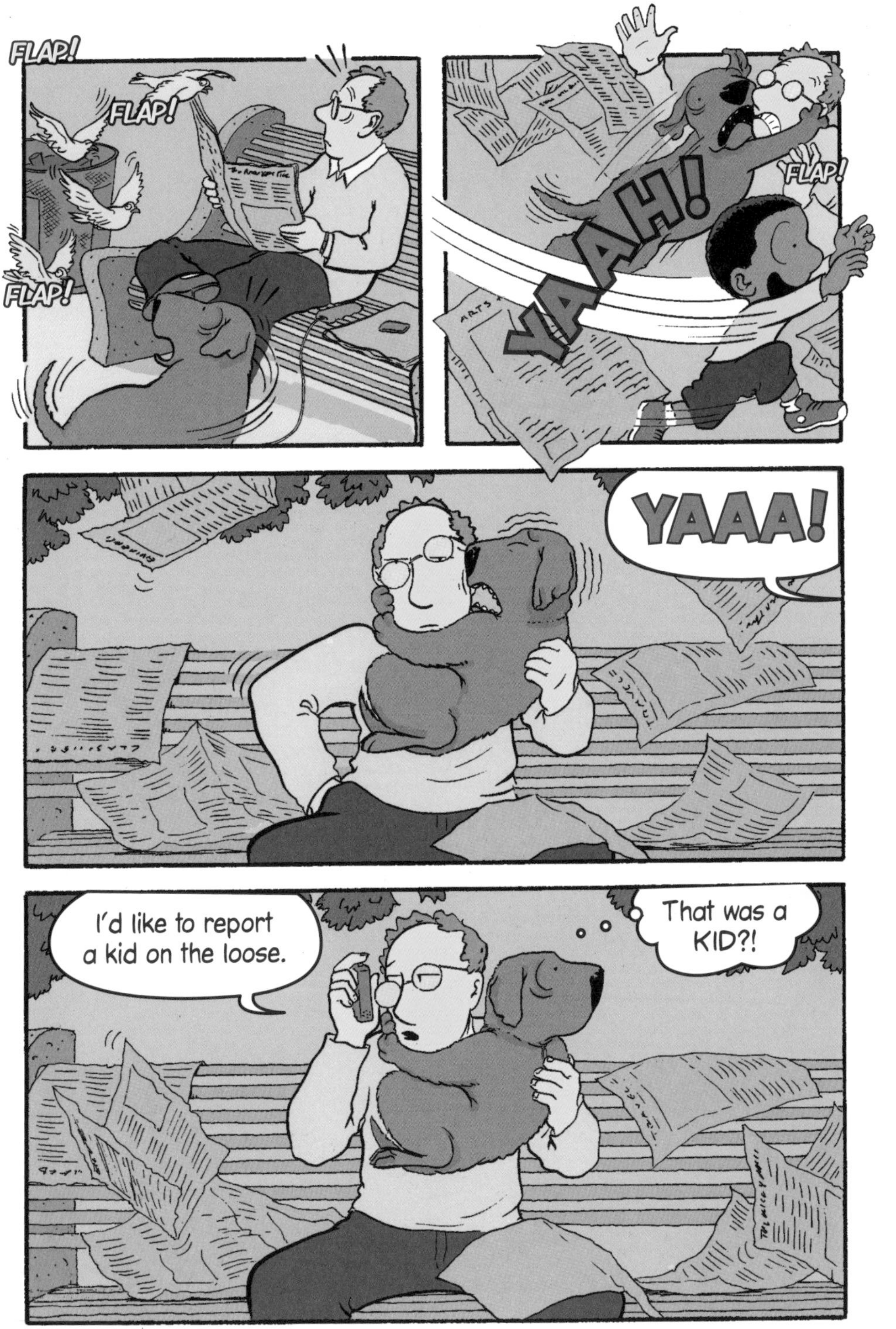
FLAP!
FLAP!
FLAP!
YAAH!
FLAP!
YAAA!
I'd like to report a kid on the loose.
That was a KID?!

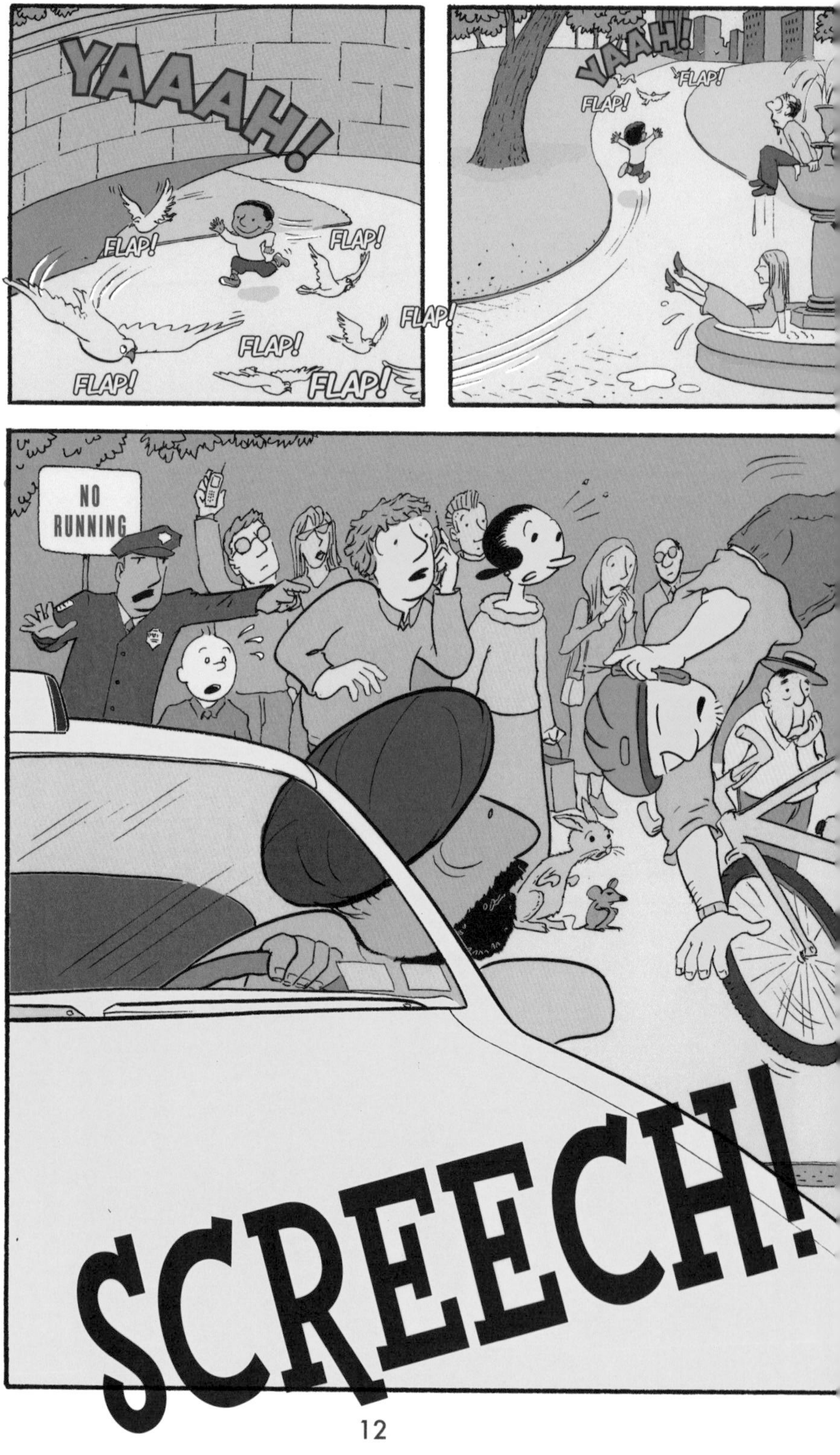
YAAAH!
FLAP!
FLAP!
FLAP!
FLAP!
FLAP!
FLAP!
YAAAH!
FLAP!
FLAP!
NO RUNNING
SCREECH!

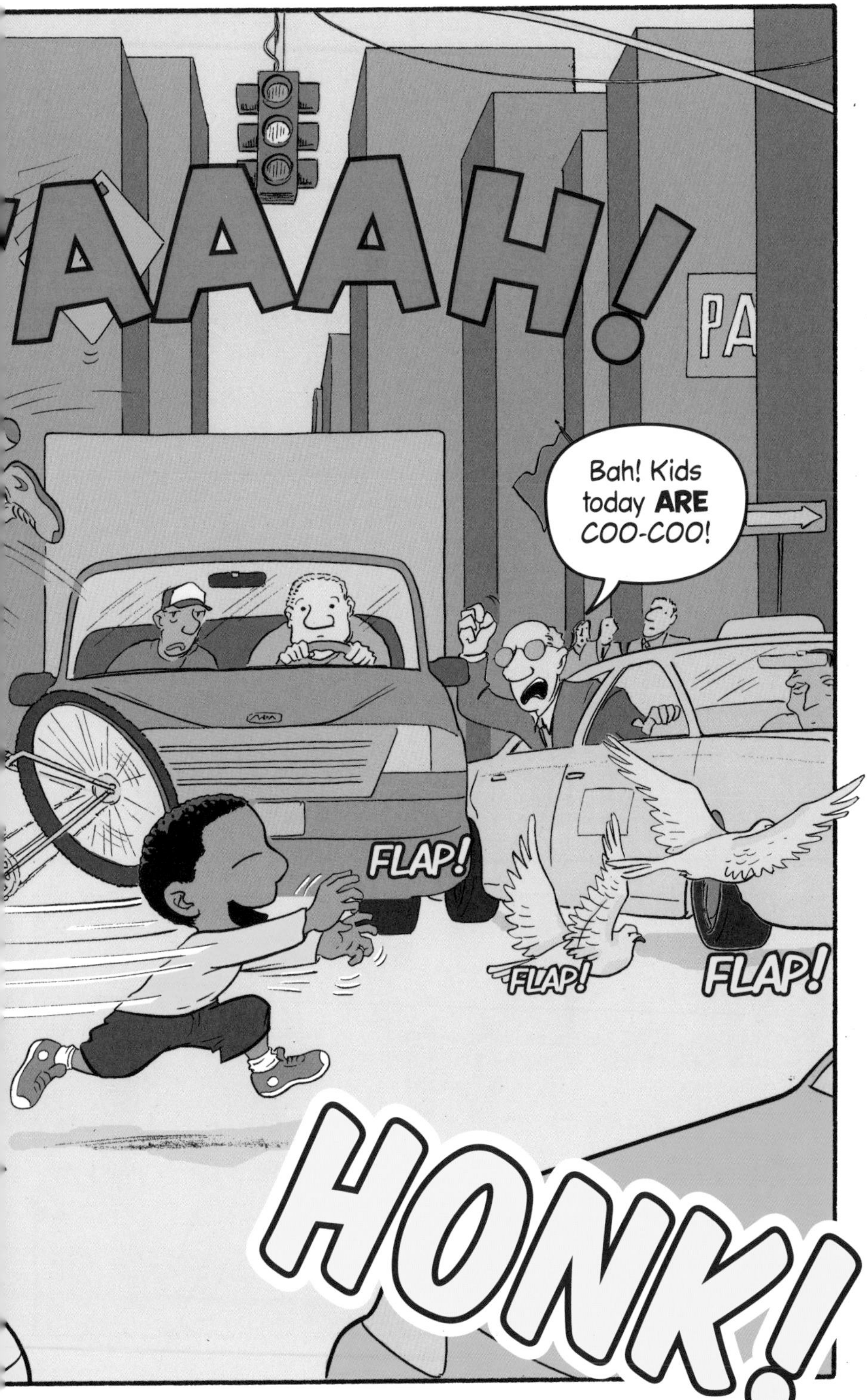
AAAH!
PA
Bah! Kids today **ARE** COO-COO!
FLAP!
FLAP!
FLAP!
HONK!

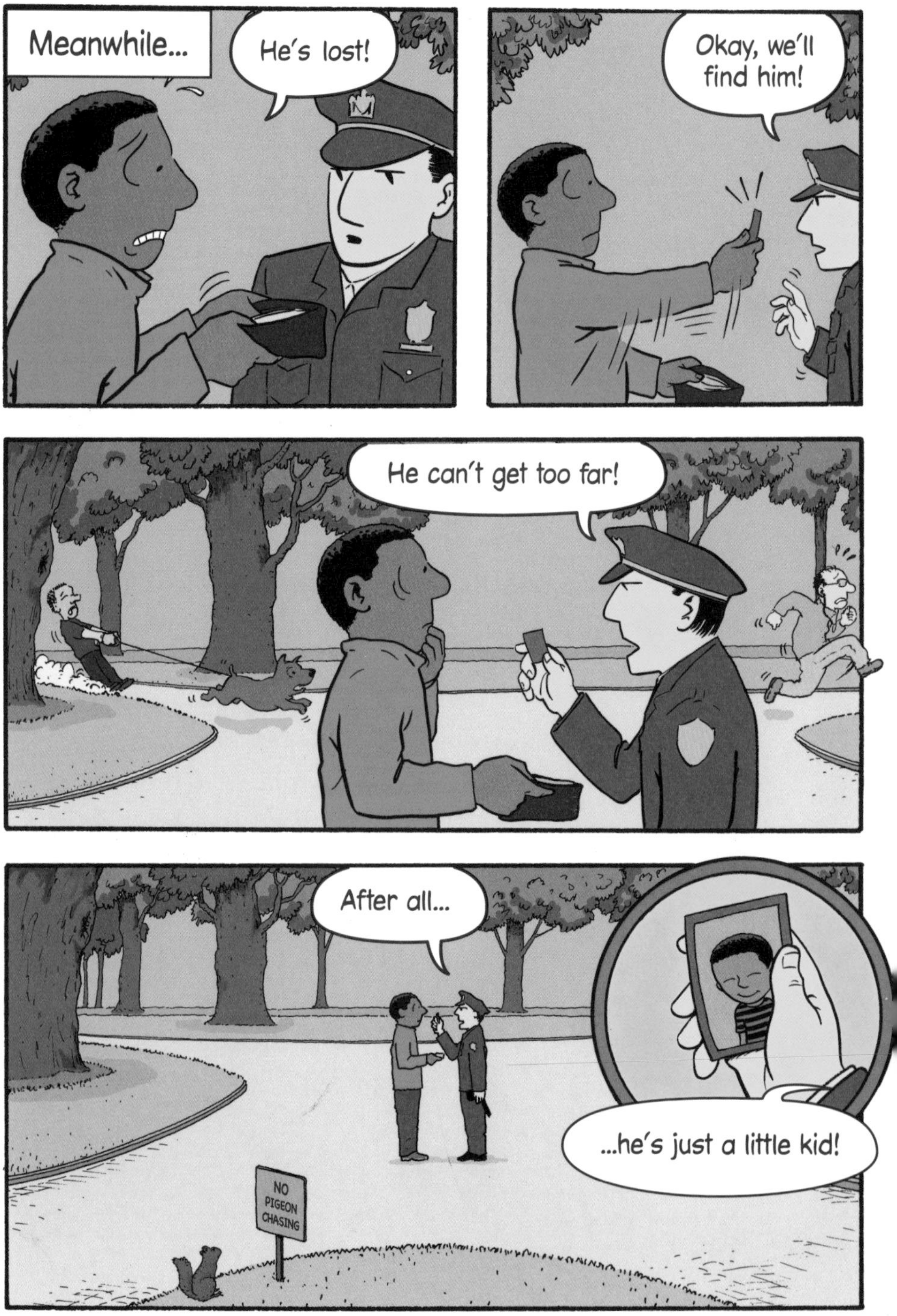
Meanwhile...
He's lost!
Okay, we'll find him!
He can't get too far!
After all...
...he's just a little kid!
NO PIGEON CHASING

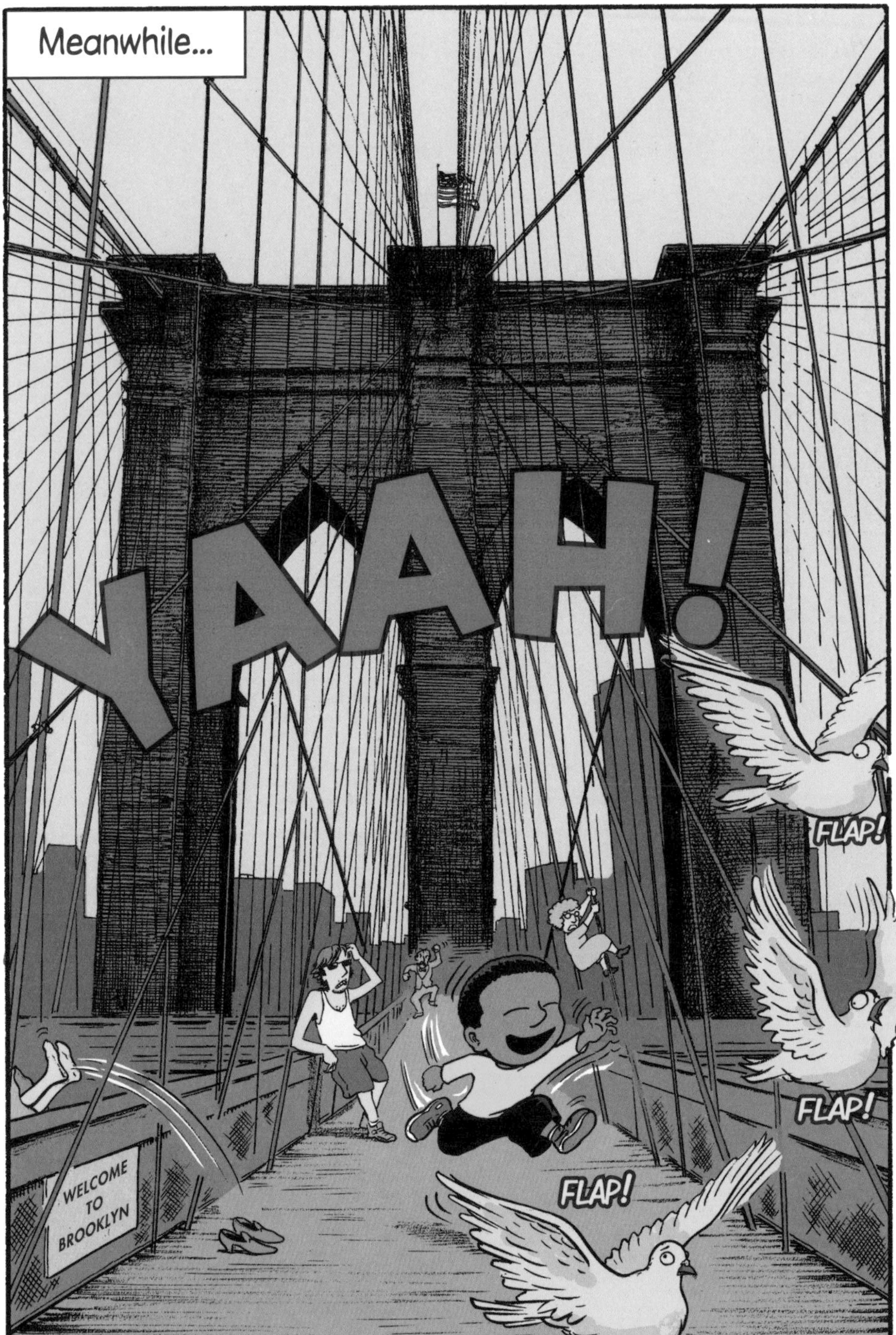
Meanwhile...
YAAH!
FLAP!
FLAP!
WELCOME TO BROOKLYN
FLAP!

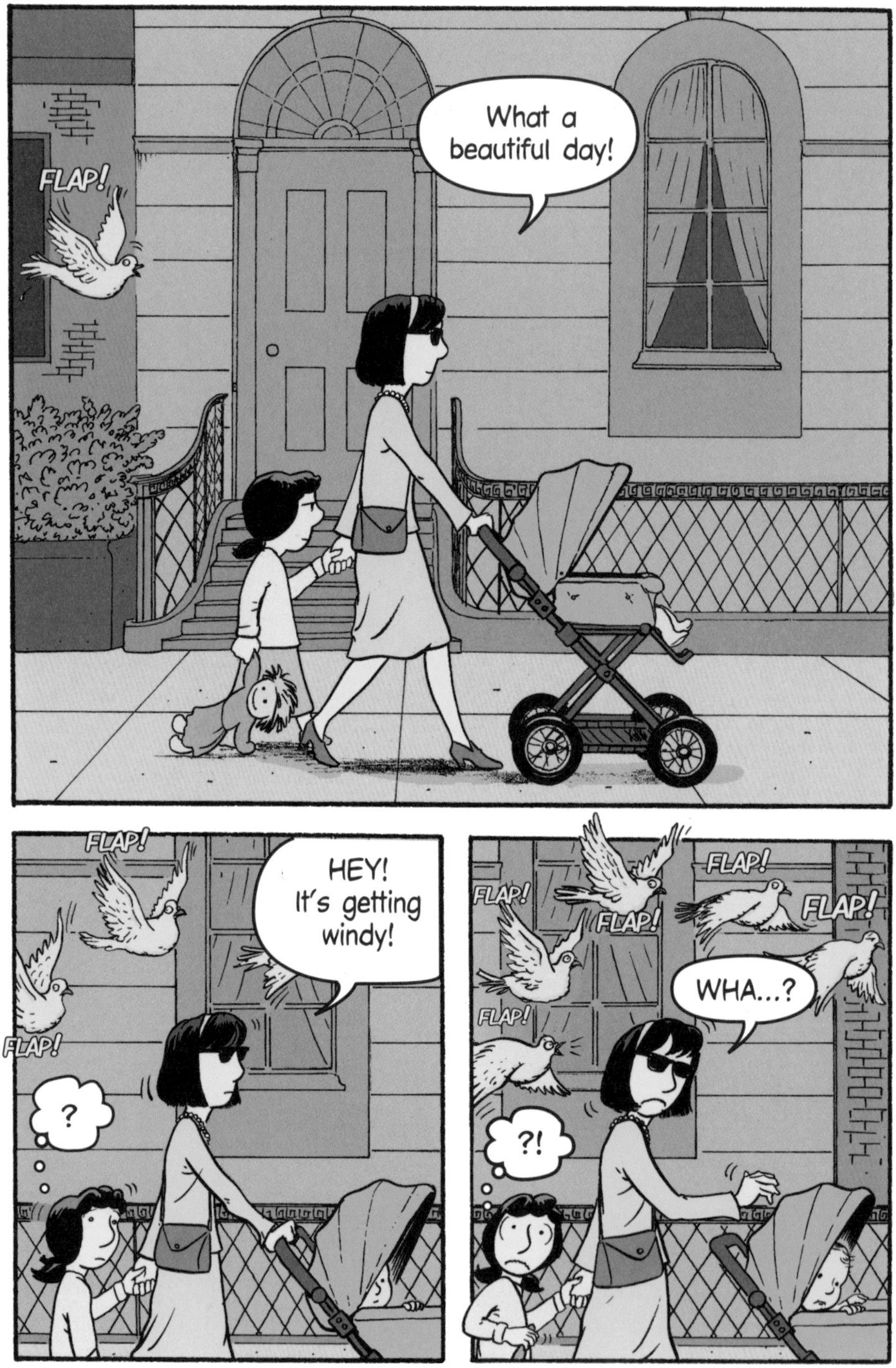
FLAP!
What a beautiful day!
FLAP!
HEY! It's getting windy!
FLAP!
?
FLAP!
FLAP!
FLAP!
FLAP!
FLAP!
WHA...?
?!

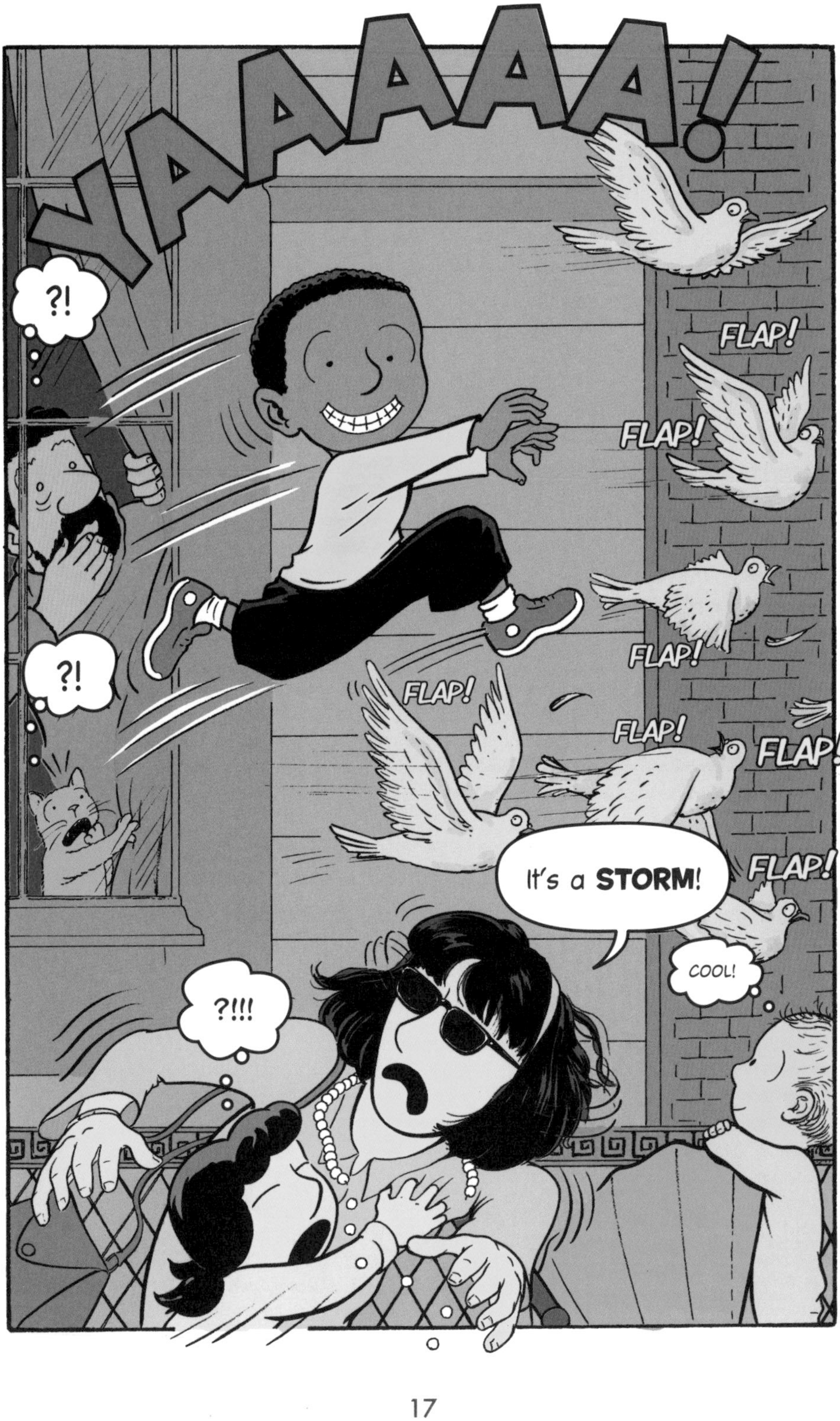
YAAAAA!
?!
FLAP!
FLAP!
FLAP!
FLAP!
FLAP!
FLAP!
?!
It's a STORM!
FLAP!
COOL!
?!!!

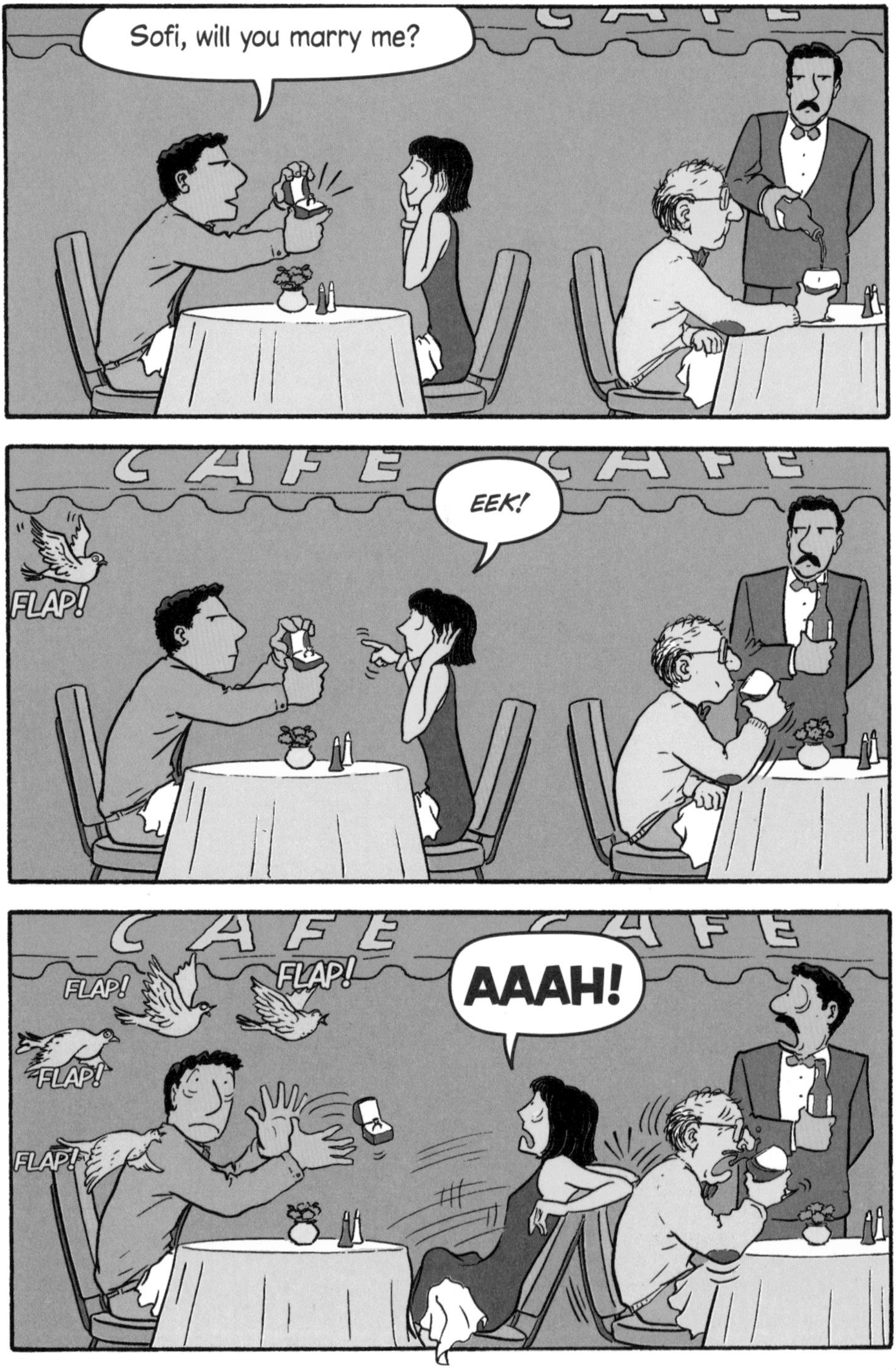
Sofi, will you marry me?
CAFE
CAFE CAFE
FLAP!
EEK!
CAFE CAFE
FLAP!
FLAP!
FLAP!
AAAH!
FLAP!

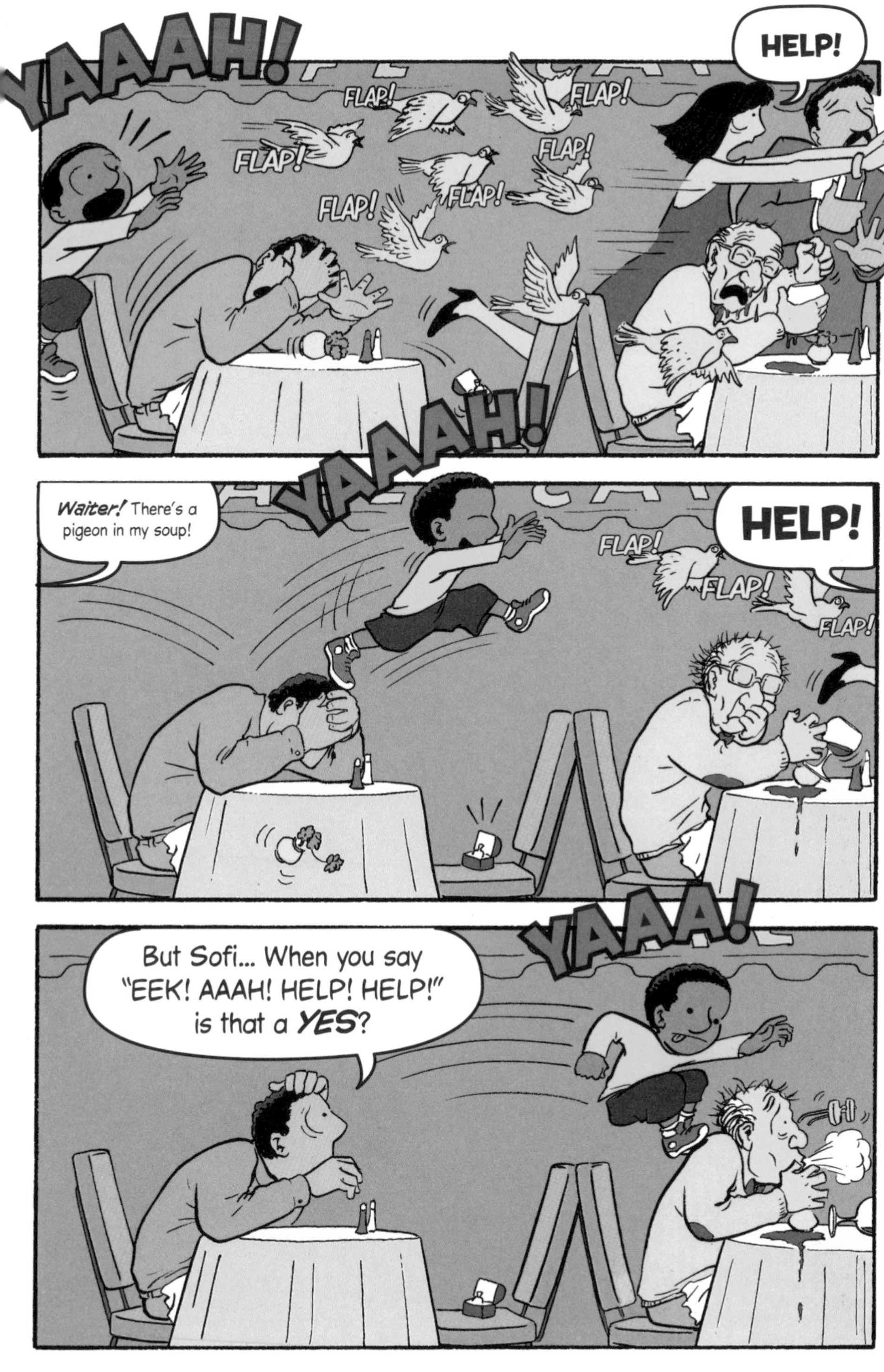
YAAAH!
HELP!
FLAP!
FLAP!
FLAP!
FLAP!
FLAP!
FLAP!
YAAAH!
Waiter! There's a pigeon in my soup!
YAAAH!
HELP!
FLAP!
FLAP!
FLAP!
But Sofi... When you say "EEK! AAAH! HELP! HELP!" is that a YES?
YAAA!

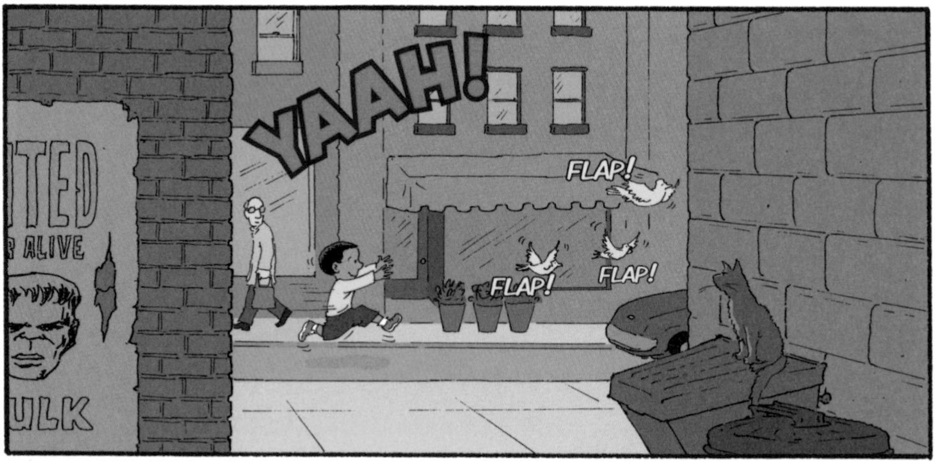
YAAH!
FLAP!
FLAP!
FLAP!

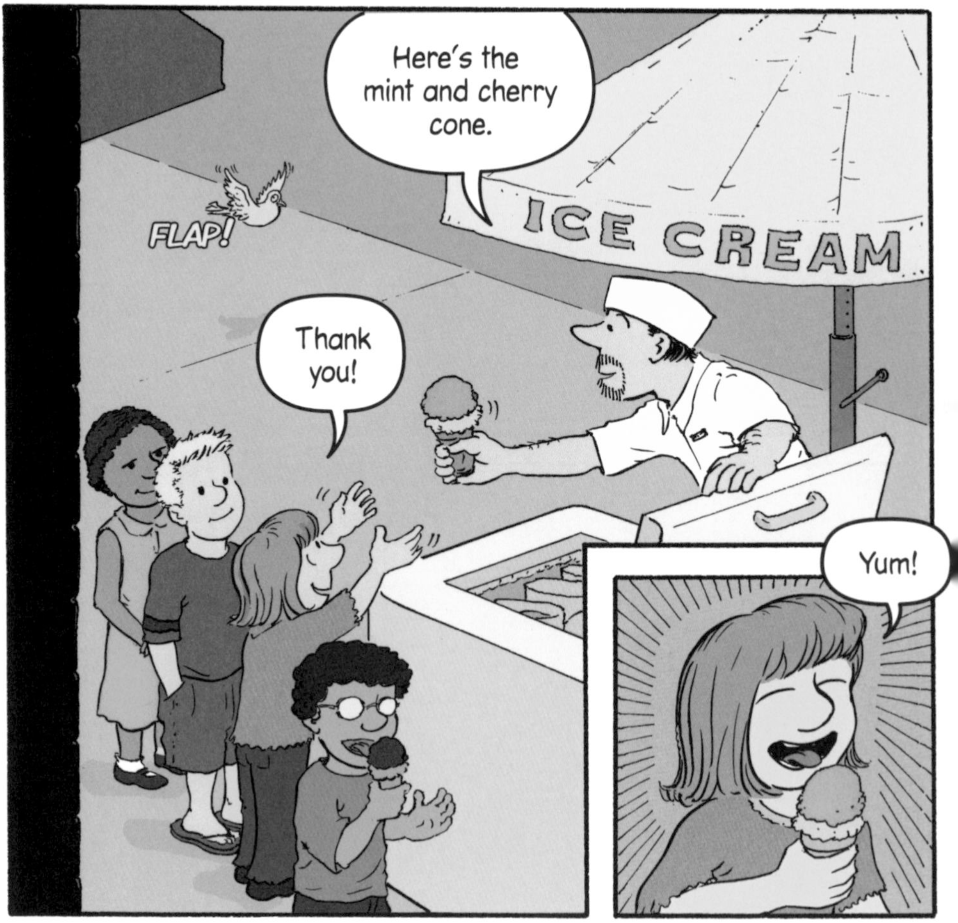
Here's the mint and cherry cone.
ICE CREAM
FLAP!
Thank you!
Yum!

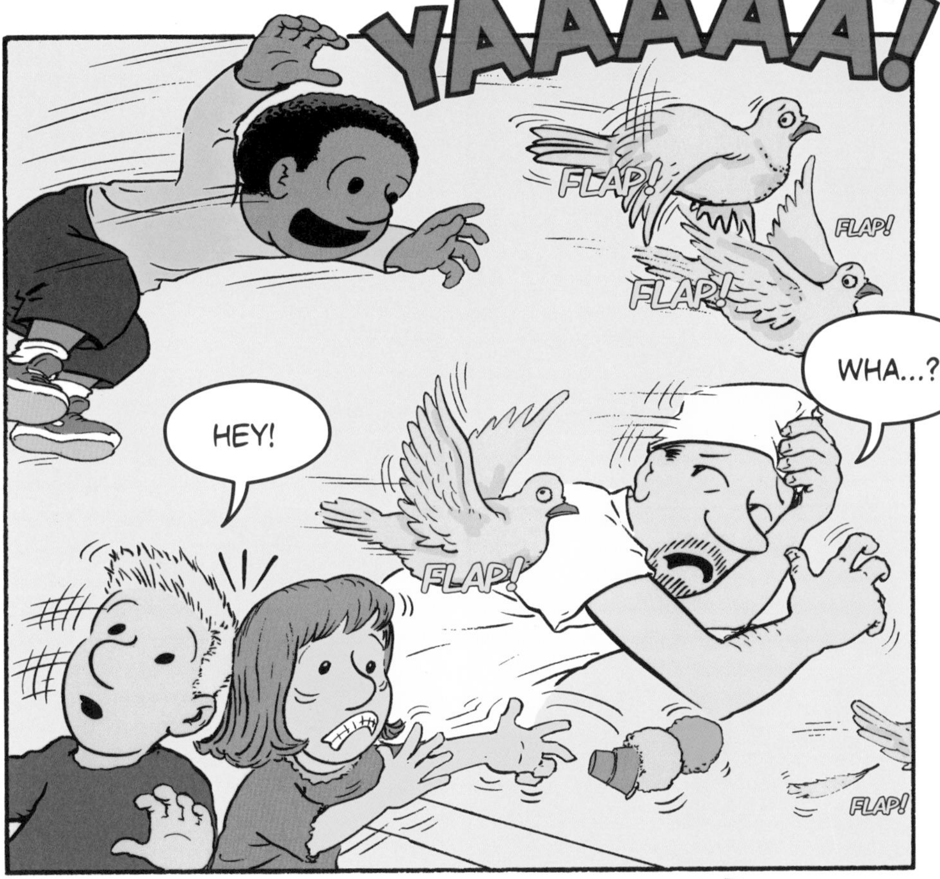
YAAAAA!
FLAP!
FLAP!
FLAP!
WHA...?!
HEY!
FLAP!
FLAP!

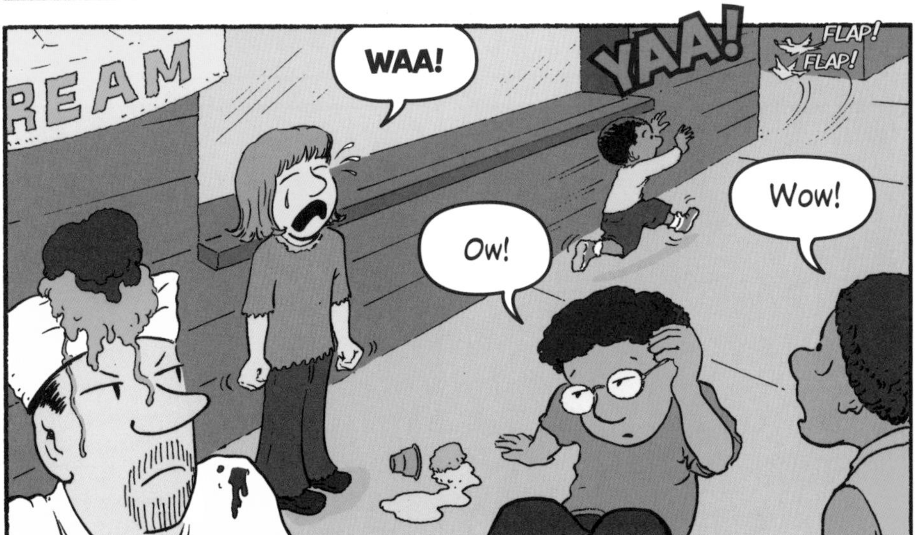
REAM
WAA!
YAA!
FLAP!
FLAP!
Wow!
Ow!

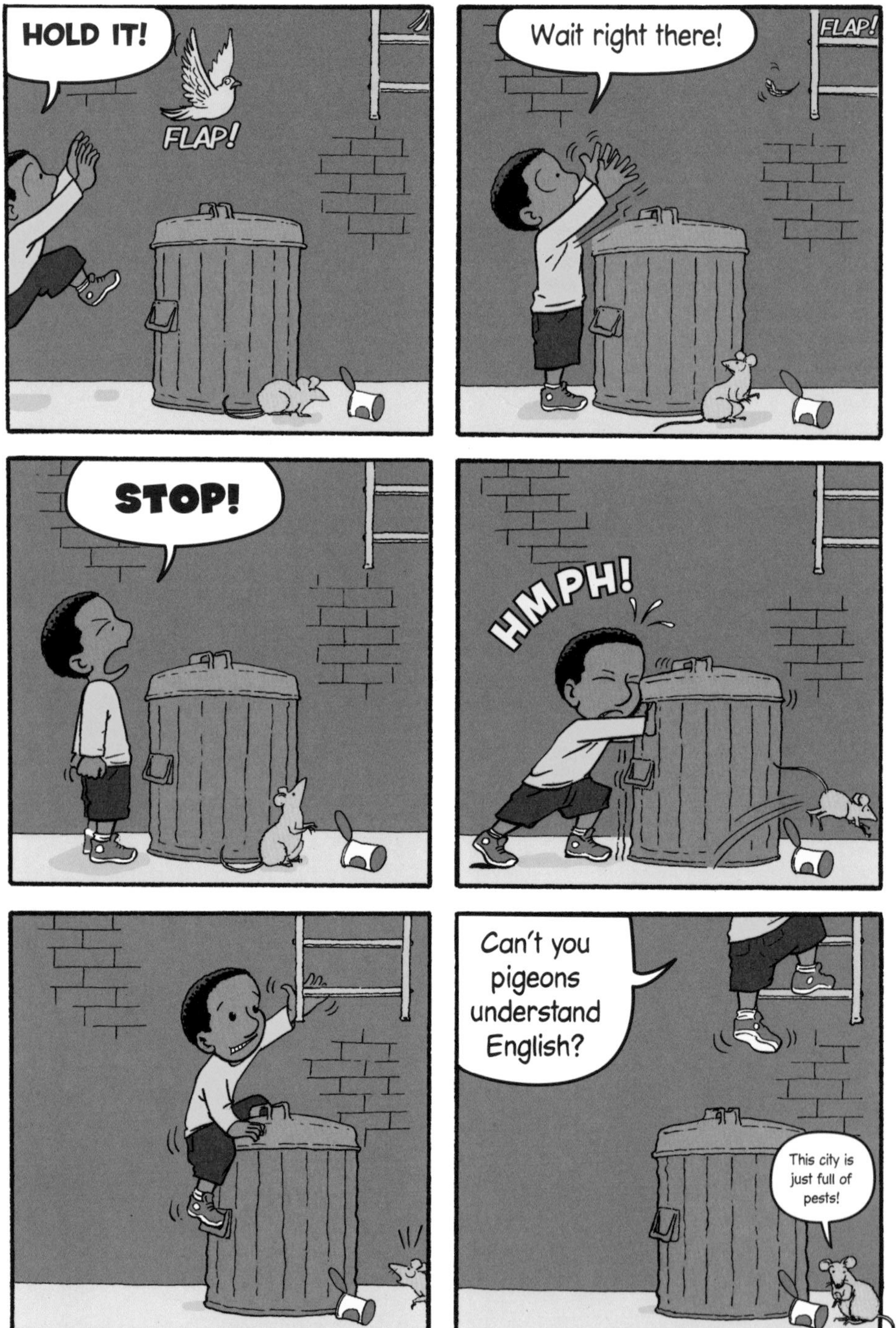
HOLD IT!
FLAP!
Wait right there!
FLAP!
STOP!
HMPH!
Can't you pigeons understand English?
This city is just full of pests!

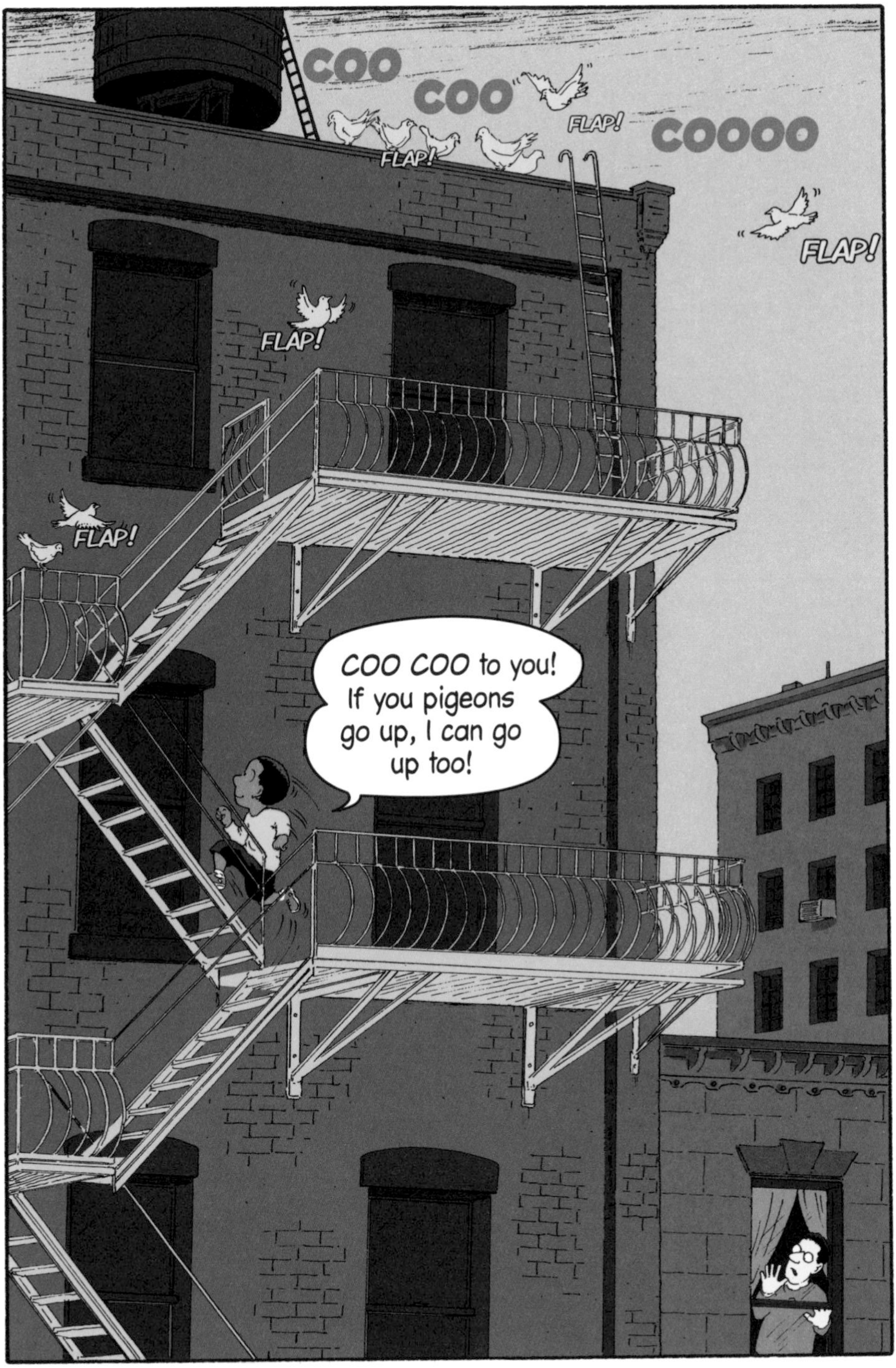
COO
COO
FLAP!
FLAP!
COOOO
FLAP!
FLAP!
FLAP!
COO COO to you! If you pigeons go up, I can go up too!

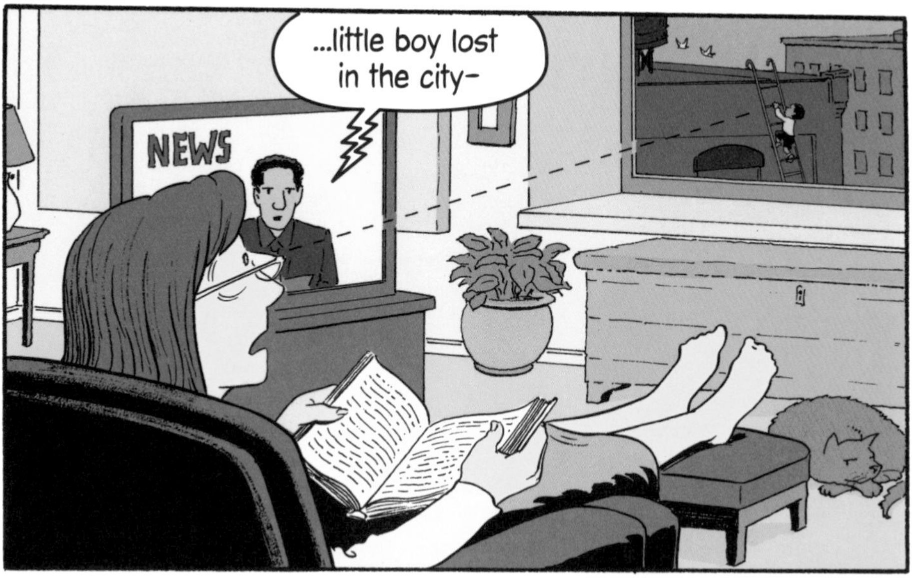
...little boy lost in the city-
NEWS

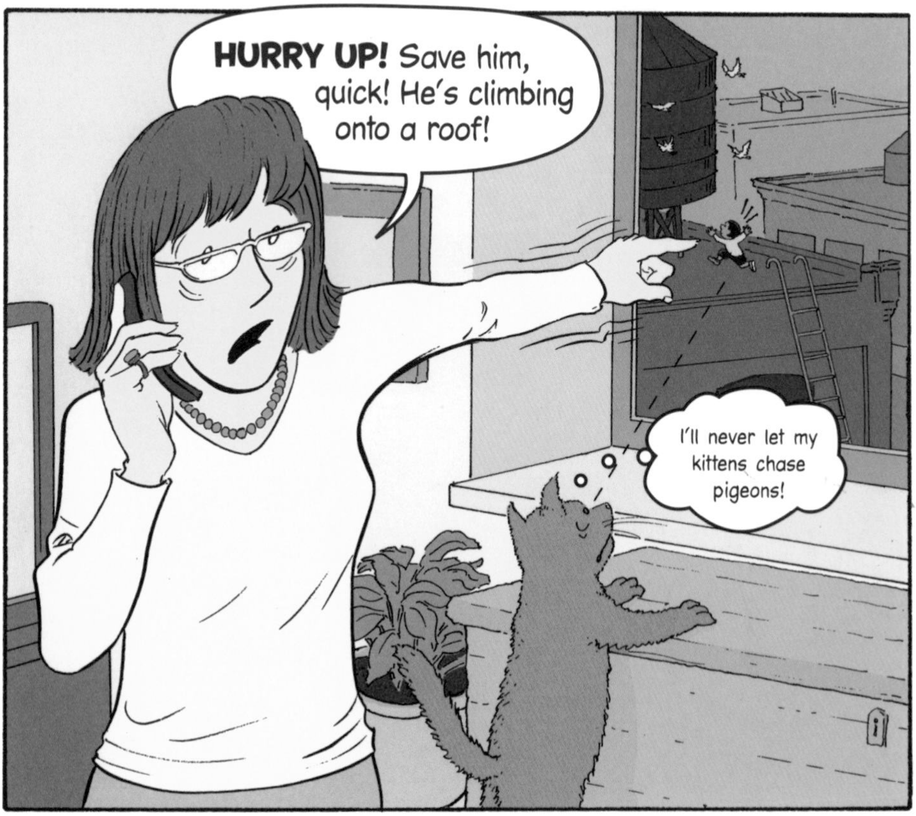
HURRY UP! Save him, quick! He's climbing onto a roof!
I'll never let my kittens chase pigeons!

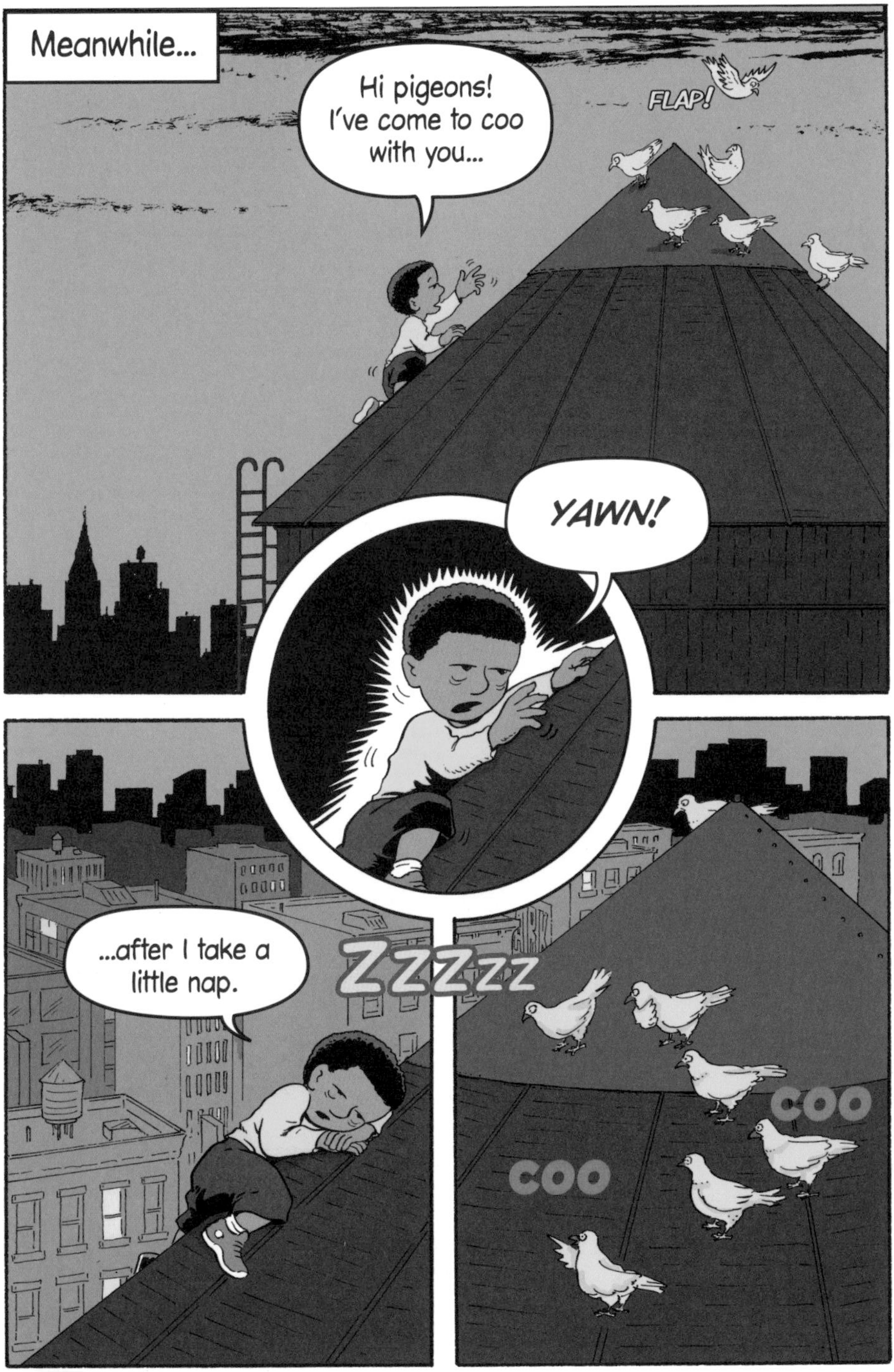
Meanwhile...
Hi pigeons! I've come to coo with you...
FLAP!
YAWN!
...after I take a little nap.
ZZZzz
COO
COO

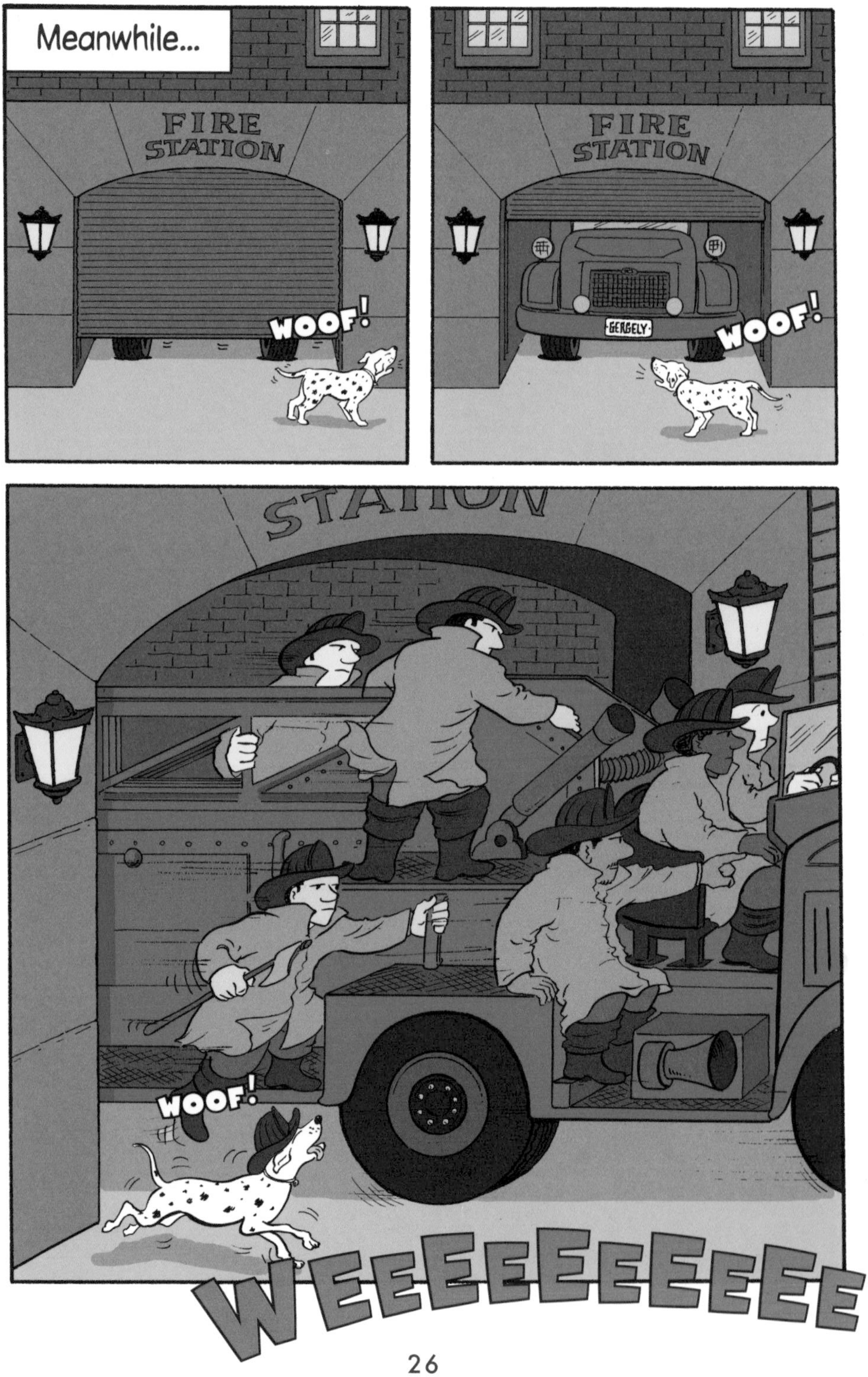
Meanwhile...
FIRE STATION
WOOF!
FIRE STATION
GERGELY
WOOF!
STATION
WOOF!
WEEEEEEEEEE

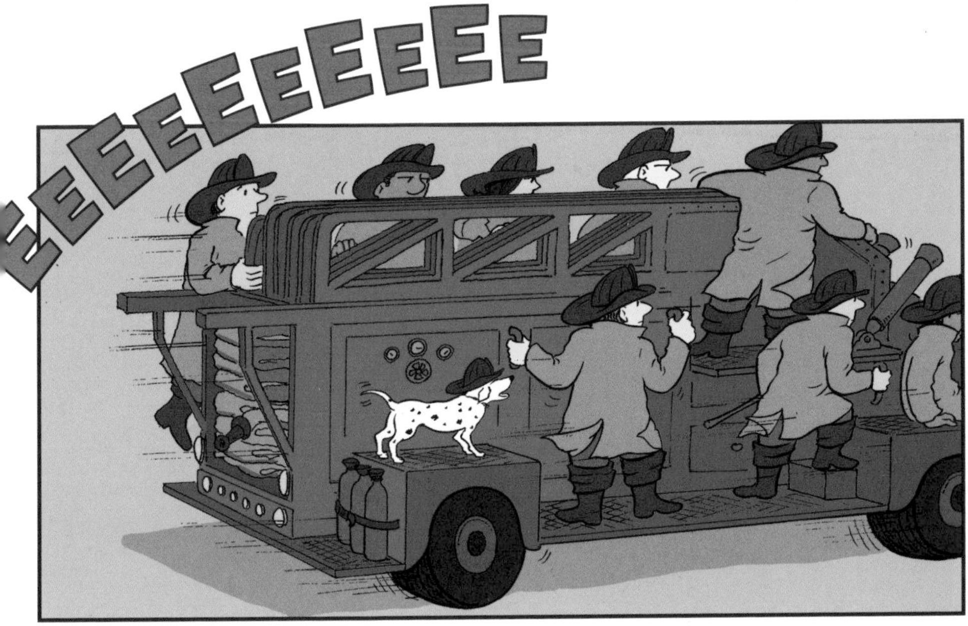
EEEEEEEEEEE

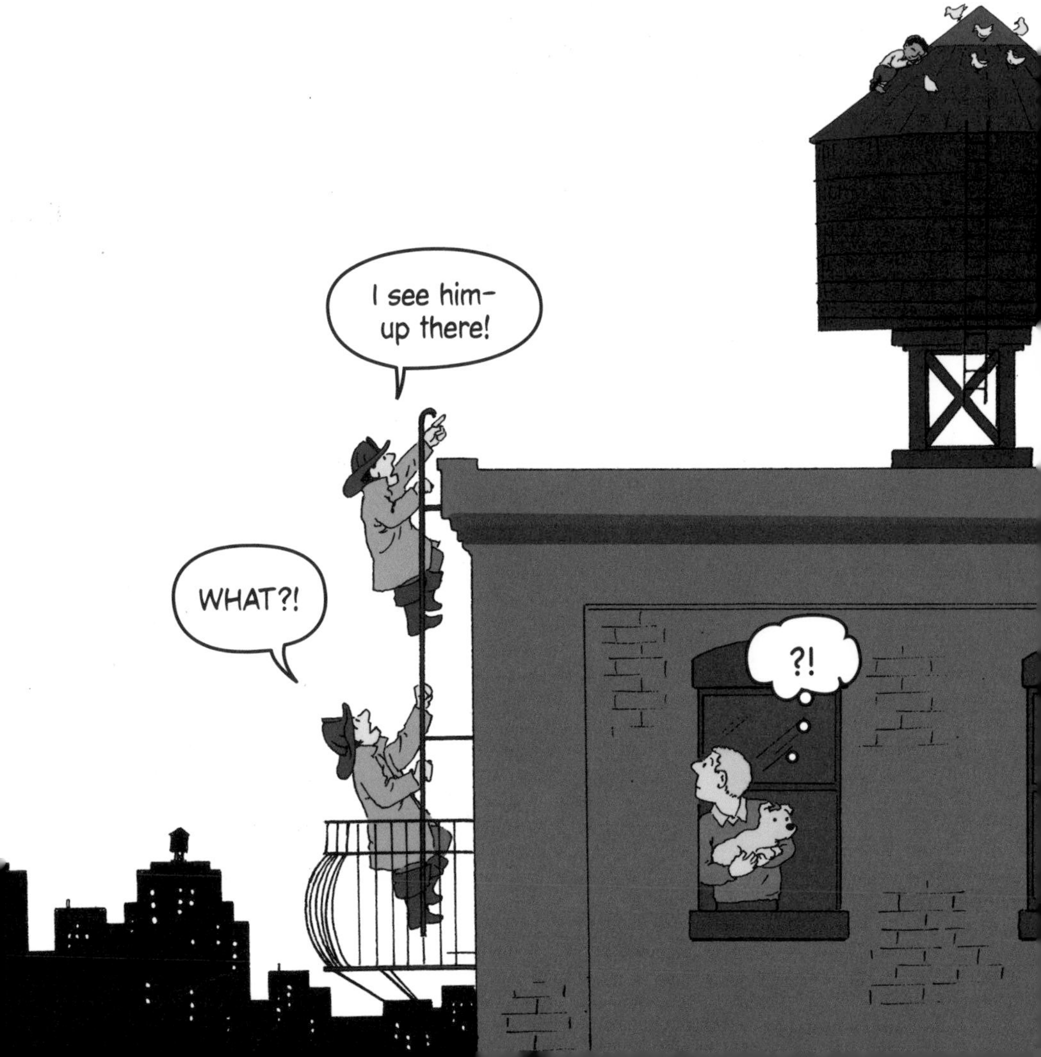
I see him-
up there!
WHAT?!
?!

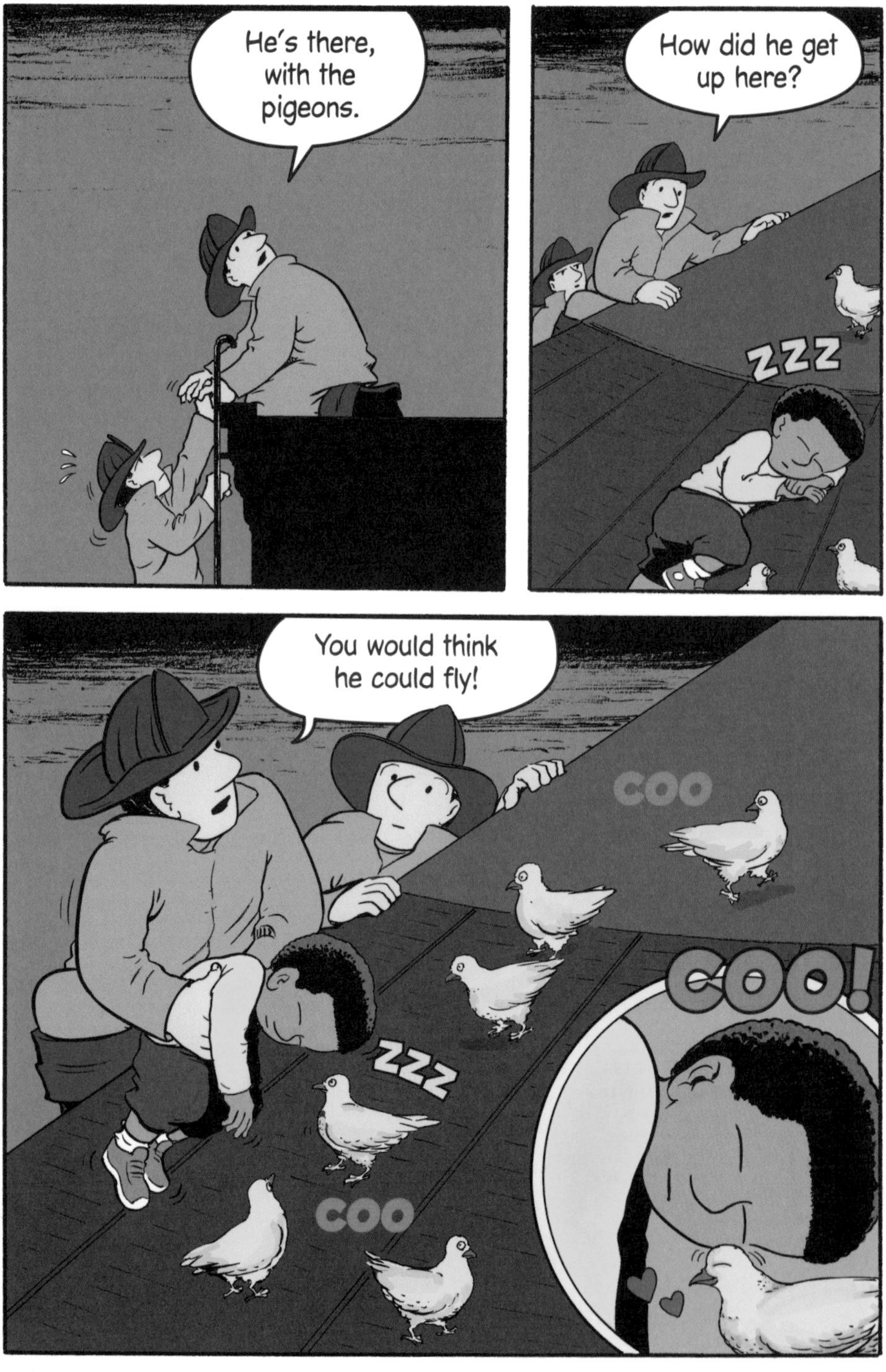
He's there, with the pigeons.
How did he get up here?
ZZZ
You would think he could fly!
COO
COO!
ZZZ
COO

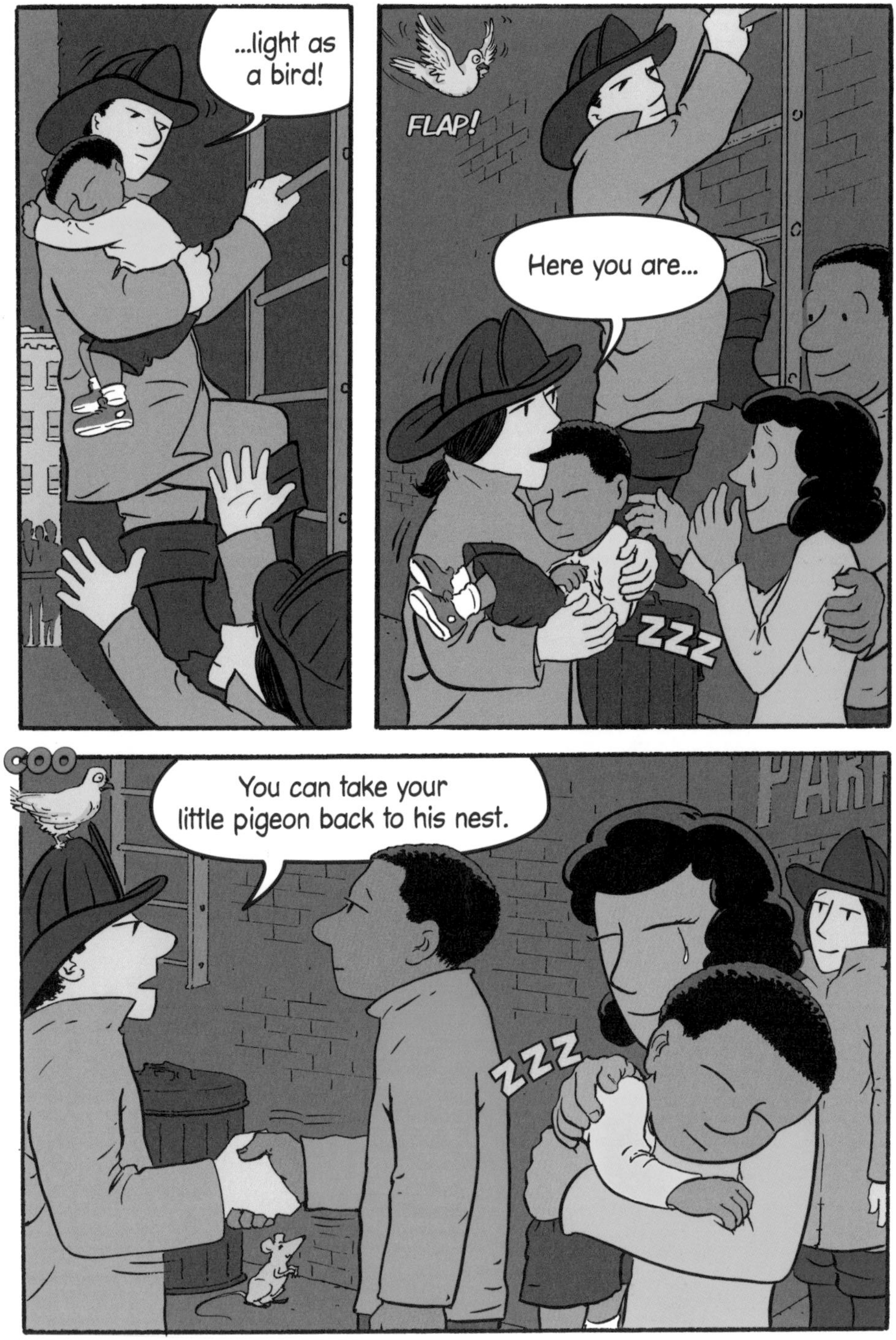
...light as a bird!
FLAP!
Here you are...
ZZZ
COO
You can take your little pigeon back to his nest.
ZZZ

And the next day...

YAAAAAA

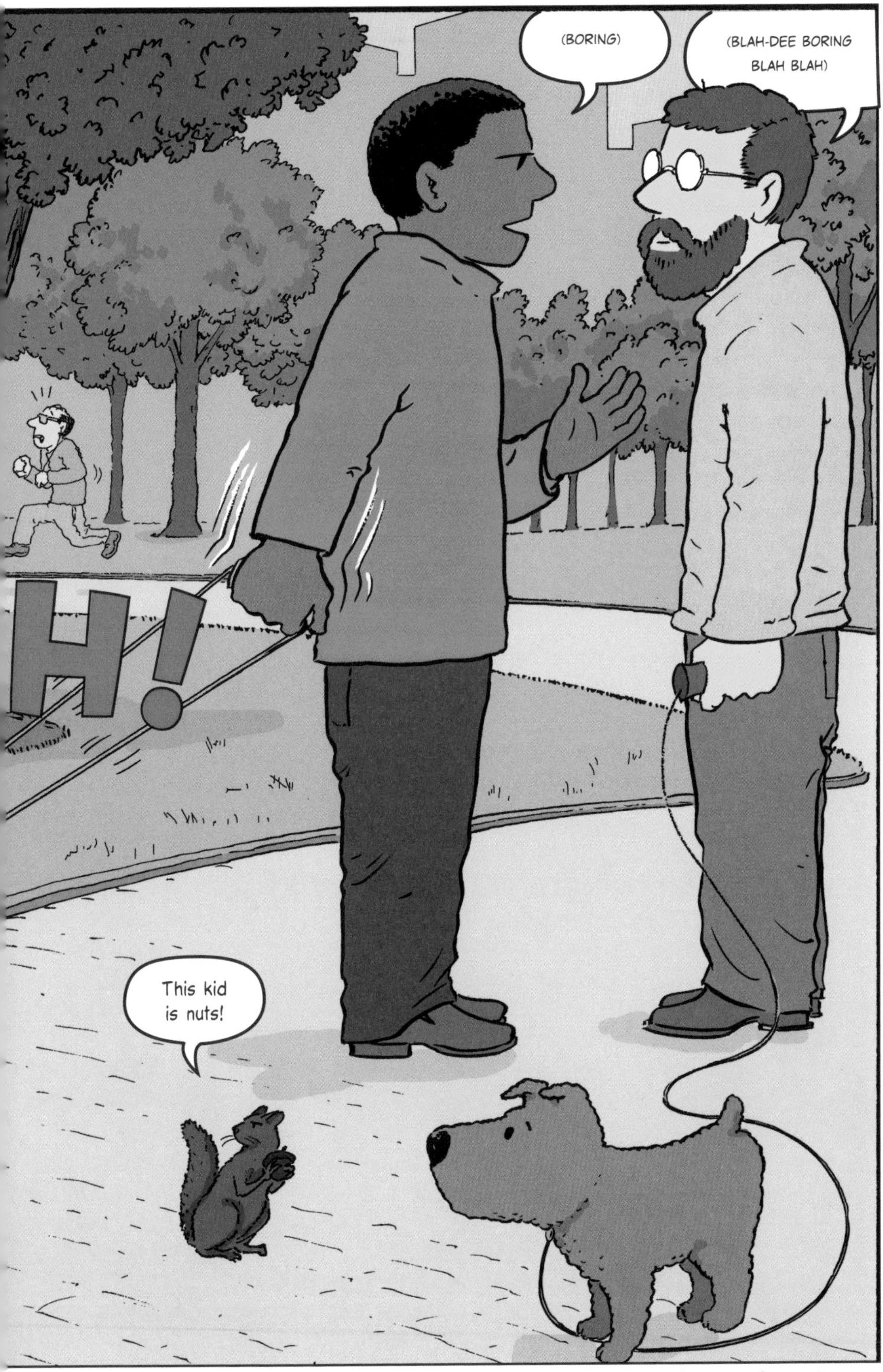
(BORING)
(BLAH-DEE BORING BLAH BLAH)
H!
This kid is nuts!

THE END

ABOUT THE AUTHOR

HARRY BLISS never chased pigeons. He grew up in upstate New York, often staying up late at night and laughing himself to sleep while looking at Will Elder's *MAD* magazine drawings. He dreamt of a life in a New York City as zany as a Will Elder panel, and was perpetually late for his school bus. Harry is now a beloved *New Yorker* cartoonist and cover artist as well as the illustrator of numerous bestselling children's books. Many of his books, such as *A Fine, Fine School* by Sharon Creech, and *Diary of a Worm, Diary of a Fly*, and *Diary of a Spider*, by Doreen Cronin, have become children's favorites. He also illustrated *Which Would You Rather Be?* by Caldecott Medal-winner William Steig, and *Louise, The Adventures of a Chicken* by Newbery Medal-winner Kate DiCamillo. This is his first comic book story.

Harry currently lives in northern Vermont with his son and their puppy Penny; Penny has yet to catch her first squirrel.